The Secrets of Pixie Hollow

adapted by
Tisha Hamilton

Reader's Digest
Children's Books®

Pleasantville, New York • Montréal, Québec • Bath, United Kingdom

Tinker Bell

Deep in the heart of Never Land is a place called Pixie Hollow. And deep in the heart of Pixie Hollow is the Home Tree. That's what the fairies call it, anyway, because it is their home. The Home Tree is full of the most wonderful and amazing magic, the kind of magic only fairies can make.

Probably the most famous of the fairies is Tinker Bell. Dressed in her emerald green outfit, Tinker Bell almost blends in among the leaves of the Home Tree, but her yellow glow, shimmering wings, and sparkling fairy dust give her away.

"Tink," as she's also called, is a pots-and-pans-talent fairy. In fact, that is how she got her name. A tinker is someone who fixes broken utensils, and Tink is the best. If it's metal and it's dented or broken in some way, Tink can fix it. She'll even shine it up until it looks better than new. Tink is a very hard worker. She won't stop until the job is done, and done perfectly.

Tink rarely goes anywhere without her tinker's hammer.

Tink made her workshop out of an old teakettle. When she found it on the beach, it was all banged up. Using the tinker's hammer that she always keeps on her belt, she carefully hammered out all the dents. She cut out the windows and doors, and turned the spout upside down to make an awning.

"You're Tinker Bell, sound and fine as a bell. Shiny and jaunty as a new pot. Brave enough for anything, the most courageous fairy to come in a long year." That's what Mother Dove told Tink when she arrived in Never Land, and Tink is determined to live up to it. She is especially fearless and ferocious when defending her friends.

If it's metal and it's dented or broken in some way, Tink can fix it.

Beck

inker Bell may be a well-known fairy, but Beck is a very talented one. That's because she takes care of Mother Dove. Beck is an animal-talent fairy. She can speak to animals in their own languages, even though she doesn't always need to. That's because her talent allows her to read the thoughts and feelings of any animal. Speaking an animal's language does come in handy, though. Beck uses it to speak with the animals and also to translate when one kind of animal needs to talk to another.

Beck prizes peace and harmony. Once, when there was a battle going on in the animal world, she helped the animals learn to be friends again. It wasn't easy, and only a fairy as talented as Beck could have done it.

Beck lives in the Home Tree.

Beck loves to play animal games, too. One of her favorites is scampering with the squirrels in a game of hide-and-seek. She also loves helping baby birds practice their flying, and she'll even play with tiny bugs. Any kind of animal is her instant friend. In fact, Beck admits that sometimes she's actually more comfortable with animals than with other fairies.

Even though her job is important, Beck never puts on airs. Instead, she is one of the most down-to-earth of the fairies. She takes her job very seriously, and the most important thing to her is to do it well. She believes in being honest and fair, and likes to do good deeds whenever she can.

Beck finds objects to help the animals.

Lily

From the tip of her daisy petal hat to the earth between her toes, Lily is a garden-talent fairy. Most fairies prefer to fly, but not Lily. She enjoys walking and feeling the ground beneath her feet. Earth is special to Lily because that's where she plants her amazing flowers. Her own garden is by far the most beautiful in Pixie Hollow.

Aside from Lily's natural garden talent, another quality that helps her grow such fabulous plants is her patience. It takes a lot of patience to plant seeds and nurture young plants so they will bloom. Lily is so patient she actually enjoys watching the grass grow.

While she gardens, Lily is often accompanied by her good friend Bumble. Lily and Bumble have tons of fun together, whether they're working on the ground or buzzing around in the air. Being a bee, Bumble also helps Lily by pollinating her flowers.

Lily's talent helps her understand what's going on inside her plants. She can sense if they're happy or sad, and knows exactly what they need at all times. Working with plants gives Lily a special feeling of joy. When she sees the other fairies enjoying her garden and making use of the plants she grows, she also gets this special feeling. Lily has a generous and loving spirit.

Fira

Just as moths are attracted to light, light is attracted to Fira. Fira is the most radiant of the light-talent fairies. Her glow is so powerful it can light the entire Home Tree. Fira makes sparks fly just by snapping her fingers!

Fira also has an important job. She trains the fireflies that light the fairy world at night. This takes a lot of patience, something Fira wishes she had more of. Her natural personality is like her name, somewhat fiery, so she often says and does things without thinking them through. That's something she's always working on to improve.

The other fairies look up to Fira. Not only is she enormously talented, but she also takes the time to give advice and help others whenever she can. That's why she's such a natural leader among the fairies in Pixie Hollow.

It takes a lot of energy for light fairies to glow as brightly as they do. Fira needs to rest and recharge every so often to make sure her glow keeps shining. Sometimes it's hard for a fairy with as much pep as Fira to slow down and take it easy. But Fira knows she must, because the fairy world is depending on her.

Prilla

There are fairies who are the best at what they do, and then there's Prilla. She is not just the best, she is the only fairy with her special talent. When she first arrived in Never Land, though, Prilla didn't know her talent. That worried her, because every fairy had a talent.

Right after she arrived, disaster struck when Mother Dove's egg was lost in a hurricane. Prilla was one of three fairies chosen for the Quest to get it back. That's when her talent emerged: in the blink of an eye, she can transport herself to the mainland. There, she can see and speak with Clumsy children and encourage them to clap to keep the fairies alive. Prilla is Never Land's first and only mainland-visiting clapping-talent fairy!

Without her talent, fairies might disappear. Knowing how special her talent is makes Prilla happy. But it can also be lonely being the only member of a talent, so the other fairies make sure she feels just as welcome in their talents.

Prilla likes to wear her faux-mouse slippers.

It's not unusual to see Prilla turning cartwheels and somersaults. She is very acrobatic and is almost always in some kind of exuberant motion. Her freckled face is often lit by a merry smile, and her good intentions mostly make up for her rookie mistakes. One of Never Land's newest fairies, Prilla is still learning the ropes.

Prilla is the one and only mainland-visiting clapping-talent fairy.

Vidia

*E*ven in a place as magical and special as Pixie Hollow, things don't always go smoothly. That's especially true whenever Vidia is around. Vidia is a fast-flying-talent fairy, the fastest one of all. Unfortunately, she's also the meanest and greediest of the fairies, too.

There's an old expression, "If you can't say something nice about someone, then don't say anything at all." If Vidia believed that, she would never open her mouth. Her sharp tongue and mean spirit had always made her one of the least popular of the fairies. Then she did something that made everything even worse for her.

Fairy dust is made from Mother Dove's feathers after they molt, or fall out as new feathers grow in. Vidia heard that fairy dust made from fresh feathers was more powerful. So in her selfish desire to fly even faster, she dared to sneak in and pluck some from Mother Dove!

The fairies didn't like Vidia before her theft. Now they don't trust her, either. Queen Clarion was so concerned she forbid Vidia to ever be in the presence of Mother Dove again.

The Home Tree is not "home" for Vidia, either. She lives by herself in the sour-plum tree. Does Vidia really like to be by herself or is she just pretending? The other fairies don't care. They're just glad they don't have to see very much of her!

Vidia lives by herself in the sour-plum tree.

Rani

*R*ani is an enthusiastic water-talent fairy. She did a brave and daring thing no fairy has ever done before. Fairies can't swim, because their wings would fill with water and drag them down. They don't even like getting their wings wet in the rain. As one of the fairies on the Quest, though, Rani needed to dive into Mermaid Lagoon. So she asked Prilla to cut off her wings.

Now, a fairy's wings can't feel pain, so it didn't hurt when Prilla cut them off, but they can't grow back either. Rani is not sorry about losing her wings, because she'd always wanted to be able to swim. Being the only fairy unable to fly sometimes makes her feel a little…left out, though.

There's way more to Rani's talent than swimming, however. She can also do the most amazing things with water. She can mold water into shapes as if it were clay. She can even bounce it as if it were a ball. In fact, if it has anything to do with

Rani's house is made of a shell just like this one.

water, Rani can help. She sometimes helps the fairies enjoy a tea party by making the water boil faster.

Rani describes herself as being "as full of water as a watermelon." That is why she cries and perspires so easily, and why her nose is often runny. Her many pockets are always stuffed with leafy handkerchiefs to soak up the excess water.

Bess

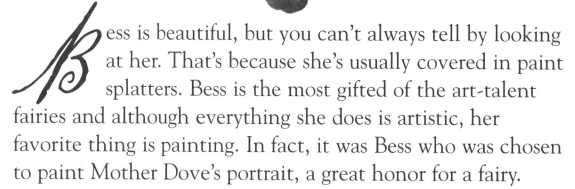

Bess is beautiful, but you can't always tell by looking at her. That's because she's usually covered in paint splatters. Bess is the most gifted of the art-talent fairies and although everything she does is artistic, her favorite thing is painting. In fact, it was Bess who was chosen to paint Mother Dove's portrait, a great honor for a fairy.

Bess finds artistic inspiration in absolutely everything—a drop of water on a leaf or a scrap of cloud in the sky. Because of this, her clothes and face are often hidden beneath a riot of differently colored paint drops. Bess doesn't care. Her art is more important to her than her appearance.

Bess loves sharing her talent, whether it's showing her artwork to other fairies or helping to decorate something for someone. Like many creative people, though, she can be sensitive, and is easily hurt if someone doesn't like her artwork.

Terence

Terence is a sparrow man whose talent is dust—fairy dust, that is. Terence is in charge of all the fairy dust in Never Land, the sparkly powder the fairies need in order to do magic or fly. Terence keeps track of it and measures it out to each fairy. This makes him so dusty he twinkles.

Terence has a crush on Tinker Bell, though she doesn't feel the same. Perhaps one day his charming smile will melt Tink's heart, but until then he must accept his role as Tink's trusted friend.

Terence hands out a cupful of fairy dust a day to each fairy in Pixie Hollow.

Dulcie

Of all the many fairy talents, the most delicious one is the baking talent. And the baking-talent fairy who bakes the most delicious treats is Dulcie. Her talent is so strong that anything she bakes will be the best. Her specialties are savory melt-in-your-mouth poppy puff rolls, but even plain bread tastes like a slice of heaven when Dulcie makes it. Her name even means "sweet and delicious." As generous as Dulcie is with sharing her scrumptious creations, she can also be bossy, especially where her talent is concerned. It's best to stay out of her kitchen while she's baking.

Queen Clarion

ueen Clarion rules the fairies with kindness and wisdom. She believes in keeping an open mind and an open heart, and no matter what the trouble is, she will calmly and gently lead the fairies to the right solution. Her deep gaze alone is often enough to get to the bottom of things. The fairies are devoted to their dear queen and would do anything to please her.

Queen Clarion believes in keeping an open mind and heart.

Decorating Your Fairy Wings

Just as there are no two fairies with the same talent, so, too, each fairy has her own distinctive set of fairy wings. No fairy has wings that look exactly like any others.

To make your very own fairy wings, use one of the ideas shown here, or make up your own design. After you're finished, you can have fun in your own pretend fairy land. Here are some ideas:

- *Turn on pretty music, put on your fairy wings, and dance like you're at the Annual Pixie Hollow Fairy Ball.*

- *Put on your wings, pretend you're the newest fairy in Pixie Hollow, and introduce yourself to the other fairies.*

- *Imagine you're at tea in the Home Tree with your new wings on, telling the other fairies about your special talent.*

- *Dress up in your favorite fairy clothes, put your wings on, and ask someone to take your picture.*

Garden Fairy Wings

Attach flowers to the center band, then put jewels and appliqués around the wings. Glue ribbons to the bottom.

Materials

What you'll need:

Waxed or parchment paper*
Scissors
Glue

Lay waxed or parchment paper beneath the wings before you get started to make sure the glue won't stick to your work surface.

If you prefer, you can ask an adult to sew the ribbons and flowers in place.

Flutter Fairy Wings

Glue four ribbon bows to the top part of the wings, then apply your favorite appliqués to the center of the bows. Attach a variety of appliqués to the center band.

Flowery Fairy Wings

Attach two ribbon streamers to your fabric flowers and then place the flowers at each of the two top corners of the wings. Glue another to the center band, and several appliqués on the wings themselves.

Bejeweled Fairy Wings

Add a row of jewels to the center band, then glue appliqués around the wings.